LEVEL 2

LEGO

DC COMICS SUPER HEROES

CARNIVAL CAPERS!

P9-DNK-479

STORY BY ERIC M. ESQUIVEL
ILLUSTRATED BY SEAN WANG

SCHOLASTIC INC.

ISBN 978-0-545-86815-0

10 9 8 7 6 5 4 3 2   16 17 18 19 20

PRINTED IN THE U.S.A.   40
FIRST PRINTING 2016

BOOK DESIGN BY ERIN MCMAHON

BENEATH WAYNE MANOR LIES THE BATCAVE, SECRET HEADQUARTERS TO BATMAN AND ROBIN!

OH NO! WHAT COULD THAT SOUND BE? IS THE DYNAMIC DUO IN TROUBLE?

"YOU CAN'T <u>ALL</u> BE ON FROSTING DUTY," BATMAN SAYS. "YOU HAVE TO PRACTICE WORKING TOGETHER AS A TEAM! TEAMWORK IS <u>MORE POWERFUL</u> THAN ANY GIZMO IN YOUR UTILITY BELT."

ALFRED HAS AN IDEA! "PERHAPS A BREAK IS IN ORDER?" HE ASKS. "MAYBE ROBIN AND HIS FRIENDS COULD INVESTIGATE THAT MYSTERIOUS NEW CARNIVAL IN TOWN?"

WHILE WALKING ALONE THROUGH THE CARNIVAL, STARFIRE STOPS BY A STRANGE-LOOKING RIDE.

"YOU THINK YOU'RE TOUGH ENOUGH TO RIDE THE FLOWER TOWER, LITTLE GIRL?" THE CARNIVAL WORKER ASKS.

ROBIN IS WALKING BY A DUNK TANK.
"TRY YOUR LUCK?" THE CARNIVAL WORKER ASKS.
"SURE!" ROBIN SAYS. "GET READY—I'VE GOT
PRETTY GOOD AIM."

ON THE OTHER SIDE OF THE CARNIVAL, BEAST BOY FINDS A DUCKY RIDE.

HOW MANY TICKETS?

THE CARNIVAL WORKER LOOKS FUNNY. "STEP RIGHT UP! STEP RIGHT UP! RIDE THE RUBBER DUCKIES!"

IT'S A TRAP! THOSE AREN'T CARNIVAL WORKERS, THEY'RE SUPER-VILLAINS!
"NOW THAT WE'VE CAPTURED YOU, WE CAN RIDE ALL THE RIDES WE WANT," THE JOKER SAYS.

BATMAN HAS A LOT OF FRIENDS HE CAN CALL ON WHEN HE NEEDS HELP! THEY'RE A GREAT TEAM.

EVEN SUPER HEROES CALL ON FRIENDS
WHEN THEY'RE IN NEED OF HELP!

THE SUPER-VILLAINS ALL SPLIT UP BUT THE GOOD GUYS WORK TOGETHER AS A TEAM!

"SORRY, BLACK MANTA, BUT THERE'S NO COTTON CANDY IN JAIL," NIGHTWING SAYS.

"NO RUNNING NEAR THE WATER!" SUPERGIRL SAYS.

SLIP!

AQUAMAN AND THE FLASH PUT
THE BRAKES ON HARLEY QUINN . . .

FINALLY, THE JOKER'S SEEING GREEN WHEN HAWKMAN AND GREEN LANTERN STOP HIS STEAMROLLER IN ITS TRACKS.

THE SUPER-VILLAINS ARE ALL TIED UP!